T0381138

# Unlikely Amigos

Susan Ten-Kate

Archway Publishing books may be ordered through booksellers or by contacting:

Archway Publishing
1663 Liberty Drive
Bloomington, IN 47403
www.archwaypublishing.com
844-669-3957

Because of the dynamic nature of the Internet, any web addresses or links contained in this book may have changed since publication and may no longer be valid. The views expressed in this work are solely those of the author and do not necessarily reflect the views of the publisher, and the publisher hereby disclaims any responsibility for them.

Any people depicted in stock imagery provided by Getty Images are models, and such images are being used for illustrative purposes only.
Certain stock imagery © Getty Images.

Credit to Illustrator: Ken Hoskin of Archway Publishing

ISBN: 978-1-6657-6130-7 (sc)
ISBN: 978-1-6657-6131-4 (e)

Library of Congress Control Number: 2024912486

Print information available on the last page.

Archway Publishing rev. date:  10/11/2024

This is a story based on real beings
who became unlikely amigos
through the power of their quest.

A crocodile lives in a beautiful sanctuary on the edge of a jungle near the cool of the sea, but his story did not begin here. It started years back when he lived as a pet in a tiny aquarium in a man's home. The man lived in a small pueblo and thought it a grand idea to have a crocodile as a pet. The man soon grew frustrated with this and felt his pet crocodile was ill-tempered. And for that reason, he named him Diablo. The man did not understand that Diablo longed to see blue skies and warm himself on a sunny rock and cool himself in a shallow pond and chat all day with, well, anyone who might lend and ear. Alas, day after day Diablo lived in a cramped aquarium that the man placed on the top shelf in his sala—far from any windows or glimpses of the sky.

When the man fed Diablo, the croc was snappy and glared at the man, and the man became frightened. He thought, *You ungrateful croc! I feed you and give you fresh water; what more could you want?* Oh, if only the man knew.

One day, the man felt he had had enough, and he carried the heavy aquarium, with the snappy croc, out of his house and into his car, and he drove a very long way to a place where he could leave Diablo. The man drove many towns away over very bumpy roads, sloshing and jostling poor Diablo around. The air was filled with stinky car fumes; Diablo felt queasy. The frog he had eaten that morning wanted to slip back up and out. Diablo did not try to hold him back. Out popped the frog, and at his first opportunity, the frog hopped out of the car window in search of a cool pond. "Goodbye, frog," said Diablo longingly. He closed his eyes tightly and felt very, very sad. Real crocodile tears began to flow.

Hours and hours rolled by, and Diablo noticed the smell in the air had changed. *Where am I?* wondered Diablo. He began to worry. The man did not understand Diablo or any crocodile, for that matter; how would he know where to bring Diablo? What if the next place was even worse?

Diablo began to chastise himself. *Why did I have to be so snappy? I could have been nicer; after all, the man did always feed me and gave me clean water, it wasn't so bad was it?* Diablo began to tremble. *Oh please, dear Gaia*, he prayed, *let my fate have a smile. Give my story a happy place for my heart.*

Diablo began to focus again on the smell; the air was sweet and salty. It was a hopeful smell, yet Diablo did not know why.

Suddenly the car came to an abrupt halt. The water in the aquarium sloshed so much that most of it sloshed out into the man's car.

Diablo could hear the man talking; he heard another voice too. *Where am I?* Diablo thought. *What will become of me?*

9

Then the man grabbed Diablo out of his car and handed him to the new man, who quickly taped his mouth shut. And with that, the man from the small pueblo got back into his car and drove off without so much as a glance back.

"Oh no, oh no, oh no," cried Diablo, terrified. He looked at the new man, and into his eyes, and for the first time in his life, Diablo saw kindness.

*"Lo siento,"* whispered the man. *"Lo siento mucho."* The new man quickly carried Diablo toward a pond, and before Diablo could even look around, he was plopped into the water. It was so bright that Diablo could not even open his eyes. But the water was warm, and Diablo was exhausted. He quickly fell asleep.

He began to dream of places he had never even seen before. It was as if his spirit was awakening. He saw a jungle in his dreams, with tall trees and light glinting between the leaves, making starlike patterns all around. He felt the soft, squishy earth between his toes, and there was a cool salty breeze he could taste.

When Diablo awoke, he met the gaze of the new man.

"*Hola, Diablo, mi nombre es Miguel,*" said the new man. "If you don't mind, I'd like to give you a new name. You are quiet and shy; how about we call you Timido—Tim for short? Now Tim, let me show you your new home."

Miguel began to explain that this place was a sanctuary—a home for crocodiles who wanted to feel safe—and sometimes other creatures came to live there too.

Diablo—ah, I mean Tim—looked around. He was lying on a big rock, surrounded by clean water, and it smelled wonderful! Tim realized that while he slept, the tape had been removed from his nose.

*Oh boy, oh boy, oh boy,* thought Tim. His heart began to smile. Ever so hopefully, ever so slowly, Tim began to realize this was his new home. He slipped off the rock and into the cool water, where he stretched out to his full length and listened to the distant sound of splashing, splashing, splashing and eased into his new life.

The next day and many days after that unfolded in the same peaceful way. Tim loved to feel the warmth of the sun while he stretched on his rock. He made a game out of sliding off the rock into the cool of his very own pool. Miguel visited him almost every day. Tim would hear him coming, as he was always singing the same song, *"Ea la nana Ea la nana duermete lucerito de la mañana"* ("Hey lullaby, hey lullaby, go to sleep, little morning star"). Miguel would frequently follow up with his own version, *"Despierta despierta pequeno estrella somnolienta"* ("Wake up, wake up, sleepy little star").

And so began Tim's new life. It was good, it was healthy, and it was loving. But somewhere way down deep in Tim's heart, he knew something was missing. *How could I not be the happiest croc in the land?* he thought. *Didn't I always wish to see blue skies? Didn't I always wish for a sunny rock and a shallow pond? What is wrong with me? Why am I not fully happy?*

Slowly, as slowly as Tim's earlier thoughts that his story did make his heart smile, Tim began to remember the last part of his wish— someone to chat with.

Yes, he did see Miguel most days, and Timido did truly love him. But somehow this was different. Miguel went to his casa every evening, and some days he did not come to the sanctuary at all. Tim wanted—no, he needed an amigo. Someone to lend and ear and to chat with. Someone to care about and who cared for him.

Timido sat with these thoughts for days and days. He wondered whether he could and should be happy just as things were or whether there was anything he could do to change his life as it was.

Tim began to pay closer attention to how Miguel opened and closed the door to his pond. *Hmm*, thought Tim. *He just pops the latch up, and the door swings open. That does not seem so difficult ..*

Every day, Tim thought, *Hmm, hmm.*

After many days, Tim began to wonder about the sounds around him. What was the splashing, splashing, splashing? It was always there—sometimes quieter, sometimes so very loud, but always with a rhythm. Water rolled in closer and closer; it would crescendo to a *splash* and then grow quieter again. Again, again, and again. *Hmm*, thought Tim. *What causes this? Do I want to see it? Is it safe? Whoa, is it dangerous?* Tim stopped thinking about this for a few days; he felt very uneasy when he thought of scary things.

In the meantime, deep in the jungle, there was a tiny *tortuga*, a turtle, smaller than his brothers and sisters and shyer than his older sister for sure. She was always bossy and always helping Mother. Speaking of *madre*, she called the tiny turtle Nacho. He didn't much care what he was called; he felt he was more than this little life. He wanted to be important; he wanted to be something other than what he was destined to be here in the jungle. He would grow up, become a father, find food for all his tortugas, and then, well, become part of the soil. Nacho wanted more.

*Hmm,* thought Nacho. *How can I become more? Hmm.* He thought about it day after day after day. *I want to be more; I want to be more.*

25

So one day, he ran away, deep into the jungle, running as fast as his little tortuga legs could carry him. He left to become more. Little did the tiny tortuga know he was heading toward the ocean. Very young ones do not know the way of the world, and Nacho did not know he was heading straight toward danger.

At about this same time, back at the sanctuary, Timido had made up his mind. *Tonight I am going to lift that latch, just as I have seen Miguel do day after day, and I am going to explore that jungle and find the sound of that splashing, splashing, splashing.*

Timido's thoughts scared him as much as they excited him, but his mind was made up. So that night, after he was sure that Miguel had left for his casa and his people, his *gente*, Tim crawled up the side of his pond, toward the latch. He stretched his neck as far as he could, but he couldn't quite reach the latch.

"Oh no, oh no, oh no," cried Tim. His thoughts were racing. *It is tonight that I have to go*. The spirit in him knew it was tonight! He gathered all his strength and pushed with his back legs as hard as he could. *Just one inch more*, he thought, *just one inch more!*

Then he heard a *clink*, and just like that, the latch was up. Timido lumbered out of the pond and through the gate, and suddenly he was out of his home, the home that he loved.

He looked back toward it and said silently, "I will come back to you home; I love you."

Now Tim was moving himself toward the sound of the splash. *Am I getting closer?* he thought. *Is it getting louder?* He pushed on and on and on, feeling tired from all the excitement and from walking for so long. Timido knew he needed to keep going. He walked over logs and large fallen trees and on squishy things.

Then he stopped in his tracks. Timido heard a low growl, followed by a tiny squeak. Que? *What in this world is making these sounds?* he wondered. He looked around, and there in the jungle, only a few feet from Tim and close to the ocean shore, was a jaguar, big and beautiful. Tim was not afraid of him; he knew deep in his heart the big cat was no match for a bigger crocodile.

He also knew the big cat was looking at something else for his meal—or rather, a snack. There on the jungle floor was a very small, very scared Nacho.

The shells of baby turtles are soft for many months after they hatch, and Nacho was only five months old. That would make him an easy nibble for the *gato*.

Tim, remembering the frog during the car ride, thought, *Well, there is no time to lose*. Tim lunged forward and grabbed Nacho into his mouth and swallowed hard. The jaguar leered at the clever croc and bounded off. Relieved, Tim did a little release and out popped Nacho, completely whole.

Nacho *was* worse for the wear, however; he was covered in croc slime and certain he was facing his end. Tim realized the tiny tortuga was terrified and smiled reassuringly. But that only made Nacho more terrified, seeing all the rows of sharp, jagged teeth. Tim quickly closed his smile and began to hum the tune he heard Miguel singing every morning.

37

This left Nacho feeling very, very confused. *Que?* Nacho sighed.

Tim changed his tactic and began to tell his story, all the way back to the aquarium on the top shelf in the sala, away from any view of blue sky. Tim explained his new life and how wonderful it was living at the sanctuary. He told Nacho all about Miguel and how much he loved him, but deep in his heart, Timido was sad because of his longing for a buddy to chat with.

This settled the tiny turtle down. Nacho shared his story and explained why he had run away from his family deep in the jungle; he wanted to be more. It was at this moment that Tim had an idea: his need for a buddy to chat with could very well be fulfilled by this little amigo. Right then and there, the two amigos decided they wanted to be friends and buddies forever!

"Hop on," said Tim. "I want to show you my new home. But first let's go for a swim."

41

Down to the shore they went, Nacho riding high on Tim's head. Right into the waves they crashed, feeling the cool, salty water float them over the sand.

"Eek!" cried Nacho again, only this time as a squeal of joy. After splashing around a bit, Tim and his new amigo headed back to the sanctuary, sneaking back in just before dawn. Sliding into the pond, Tim closed his eyes with a happy smile in his heart, and Nacho found a warm rock to rest on, feeling in his heart that he was more.

43

Here they lived their days, basking in the warm sun on the rock, slipping into the cooling water when the noonday sun was *muy calor*. They chatted the hours away and retold the story of how they became unlikely amigos. And every so often, when they felt the need for a little bit of adventure, Tim and Nacho would slip out of the cool pond and head off to the beach!

45

Miguel, noticing a new friend at the sanctuary, began to bring lettuce and other tortuga treats to the pond so that these unlikely amigos could live happily ever after. And guess what? They did!

Susan Ten-Kate

Printed in the United States
by Baker & Taylor Publisher Services